¡Hola, Lola!

Dance of the Feathers

BY KEKA NOVALES

ILLUSTRATED BY GLORIA FÉLIX

PICTURE WINDOW BOOKS
a capstone imprint

Published by Picture Window Books, an imprint of Capstone.
1710 Roe Crest Drive, North Mankato, Minnesota 56003
capstonepub.com

Library of Congress Cataloging-in-Publication Data is available
on the Library of Congress website.
ISBN: 9781666337280 (hardcover)
ISBN: 9781666343915 (paperback)
ISBN: 9781666343953 (ebook PDF)

Summary: Abuelita can't visit Lola for her birthday, so she sends
her tickets to the ballet. Lola loves the show so much that she
decides she wants to be a ballerina. But dance is not as easy as it
seems. When Lola's instructor announces they'll be dancing *Swan
Lake* for their recital, Lola is excited . . . until she learns her role.
Rather than a graceful swan, she'll be a background chicken! Lola
must learn she can still be an important part of the show, as long
as she's comfortable in her own feathers.

Design Elements: Shutterstock/g_tech, Shutterstock/Olgastocker

Designed by Kay Fraser

TABLE OF CONTENTS

Meet Lola!

¡Hola, I'm Lola! I live in Texas with my family—Mama, Dad, and my baby sister, Mariana. The rest of my family, including my grandparents, live in Guatemala. That's where my parents are from. I know lots of interesting facts about the country.

Facts About Guatemala

- Guatemala is in Central America. It is about the size of the state of Tennessee.

- Guatemala has 37 volcanoes, but only three are active—that means they're erupting. The other 34 are asleep.

- The official language in Guatemala is Spanish.

Facts About Me

- I'm learning Spanish.

- I love history. I want to be an archaeologist when I grow up.

- I adore my family.

- I don't like change.

- I hate Mondays and onions, not to mention waking up early. Yuck!

My Family

Mama likes to speak Spanish at home. She is always trying to teach me about my roots and culture. Here are some other facts about Mama:

- She loves chocolate.
- She misses her family in Guatemala and wishes we saw them more often.
- She hates clutter!

Dad travels a lot for work. Since he is gone so much, our family time is extra special. Here are some other facts about Dad:

- He loves cars.
- He hates being late.
- He always makes us laugh!

Abuelita, my grandma, is one of my favorite people. She visits us once or twice a year. It is magical when we are together. She has the best stories. Here are some other facts about Abuelita:

- She cooks the best food and gives the best advice.
- She knows how to do just about anything.
- She is my favorite!

Abuelo, my grandpa, spends most of his time in Guatemala. (Don't tell anyone, but I think he is afraid of planes!) Here are some other facts about Abuelo:

- He loves Abuelita's cooking!
- He is always happy.
- He loves singing, telling jokes, and being playful.

Chapter 1

Birthday Surprise

"Happy birthday to you. Happy birthday to you . . ." My parents sang as they came into my room. Then they continued with the Guatemalan version. "Ya queremos pastel . . ."

I sat up in bed. Mariana, my little sister, crawled into bed with me and gave me a big hug.

"¡Feliz cumpleaños, Lola!" Dad said.

"Let's go downstairs to the kitchen," Mama said. "Breakfast is on the table. And we have a surprise for you!"

I ran downstairs. In the kitchen, I saw a huge tres leches cake—and presents!

"My cake!" I exclaimed. "Cake for breakfast?"

"We are starting a new tradition," Mama announced with a wink.

"Make a wish!" Dad told me.

I closed my eyes and took a deep breath. *I wish Abuelita could be here,* I thought as I blew out my candles. My grandmother lives in Guatemala. She visits us for a few months each year.

Mama handed me a box. "Open it!"

I opened my presents. I got an arts and crafts set, a sparkly pink dress, and matching shoes.

"Thank you! I love them all!" I cheered.

Mariana grabbed for my arts and crafts set.

"Can I open it?" I asked Mama.

Mama nodded. "Go ahead."

I started getting everything out of the box. Then the phone rang. Mama answered and passed it to me.

"¡Hola, Lola! ¡Felicidades!" Abuelita said.

"Thank you!" I replied. I told Abuelita all about my presents and cake for breakfast.

"That sounds like a wonderful tradition," Abuelita replied. "Oh, here comes Abuelo. He wants to wish you a happy birthday too!"

A moment later, my grandpa's voice came through the phone. "¡Feliz cumpleaños, Lola! I wish I could be there with you," he said.

"Maybe next year you can come to celebrate my birthday with me," I suggested.

"Great idea, mija! I'll pass the phone back to Abuelita. She has something to tell you. ¡Te quiero, Lola!" Abuelo said.

"I love you too, Abuelo!" I replied.

"Did you get our present?" Abuelita asked.

"Let me ask," I told her. I turned to Mama. "Mama, Abuelita says they sent me a present."

"Yes, Mariana is bringing it to you," Mama said with a smile.

Dad carried Mariana into the room. She held a white envelope. Dad was trying to keep it out of her mouth.

"Mariana, can I please see my present?" I asked. "I'll trade you for some cake!"

Mariana giggled and gave me my gift. I opened the slightly soggy envelope.

"Since we can't be there with you for your birthday, we want you to have a magical celebration," Abuelita said. "We know how much you love to dance. We sent you tickets for the afternoon show at the ballet!"

I gasped. I loved to dance! Mama and I danced around the house all the time. But I had never been to the ballet.

"We sent you four tickets. That way you and your mama can take Joy and Sophia too," Abuelita added.

"Thank you so much, Abuelita!" I said. "You're the best! And tell Abuelo I said thank you too."

"You're very welcome," Abuelita said. "Adiós, birthday girl!"

I hung up the phone and turned to my parents. "Mama, we're going to the ballet!" I leapt with joy. "Is it okay if I wear my new dress?"

Mama smiled. "Absolutely!" she said. "Joy and Sophia will be over after lunch. I cleared it with their parents when Abuelita asked me about the tickets."

I started twirling across the living room, imagining myself at the ballet. This was the best birthday ever!

Chapter 2

At the Theater

I couldn't wait to go to the ballet! After lunch, I put on my new dress and sparkly shoes and admired myself in the mirror.

I wished Abuelita and Abuelo could be here too, I thought. I always missed them the most on holidays and special occasions.

Just then, the doorbell rang. I ran to open the door. Joy and Sophia stood on the other side. They were wearing fancy dresses too.

"You both look great!" I told my friends.

"You too!" Joy said. "I love your dress."

"Thanks for inviting us," Sophia added.

"Ready, girls?" Mama asked, joining us by the door.

"Ready!" we all cheered.

Mama drove us to a theater downtown. It was beautiful! There were big, fancy doors at the entrance. Inside, there were shiny mirrors everywhere.

"Look at the stage!" I exclaimed.

Sophia pointed. "They have an orchestra!"

"Look at all the lights!" Joy said.

We hurried to our seats. Huge red velvet curtains covered the stage. I studied the program. It listed all the dancers who would be performing today.

Soon the orchestra started playing, and the theater got dark. Then the curtain went up. Joy, Sophia, and I exchanged excited looks.

The dancers paraded across the stage. Their costumes were beautiful! They wore white leotards and fluffy tutus.

I was amazed at how they stood on the tips of their toes. The ballerinas reminded me of the tiny dancer inside the music box Abuelita gave me last year for my birthday.

The show flew by. I didn't want it to end! When the ballet was over, everyone stood and clapped. I couldn't wait to tell Abuelita all about the fantastic show!

"So, I guess you liked the ballet?" Mama asked when we were back in the car.

"I loved it! I want to be a ballerina when I grow up!" I declared.

"I thought you wanted to be an archaeologist," said Sophia.

"Not anymore. The theater is calling me!" I announced.

Mama laughed. "It's great that you want to try something new," she said. "The good news is you can have lots of hobbies!"

"That's true," Sophia added. "My favorite hobbies are karate and piano."

"Dance isn't a hobby. It's my life!" I said seriously.

Joy and Sophia giggled.

"I loved, loved, loved the show!" Joy announced. "I want to be a dancer too!"

"You girls have the ballet bug!" Mama said.

"Maybe we should all take lessons together," Joy suggested.

"Mama, can we?" I asked.

"Let's slow down, girls," Mama replied. "Let me talk to your parents first. If they agree, we can look into it."

Joy, Sophia, and I all squealed.

"Fingers crossed our parents say yes!" Joy cheered.

Chapter 3

First Class

Two weeks later, it was time for my *first ever* ballet class! Mama had signed me up for classes at Madame Juliette's Dance Academy three times a week.

Sophia decided she was too busy with piano and karate, but Joy's parents signed her up for ballet too.

Joy came to my house after school to get ready. Our parents had bought us both pink leotards, pink tights, pink skirts, and pink ballet shoes. We both wiggled into our tights.

"Let's get this party started!" I cheered.

I turned on some music while we got ready. I couldn't help but dance. Joy and I both wiggled our hips to the Latin beat.

"This is salsa," I told Joy.

"You're really good!" she replied.

The last touch to complete our ballerina look was our hair. Joy already had hers in a bun. Mama helped me with mine.

"Let's go!" Mama said. She buckled Mariana in her car seat, and off we went.

"Can we listen to a Spanish station?" I asked.

"Great idea!" Joy agreed.

Mama tuned the radio to my favorite station. Joy and I danced in our seats. In her car seat, Mariana clapped and danced to the music too.

"Do you know what rhythm this is?" Mama asked.

"Salsa!" I cheered.

Another song came on. "How about this one?" Mama asked.

I hesitated. "Merengue?"

"Listen to the beats," Mama said. She started counting them.

"Bachata?" I guessed.

Mama nodded. "Great job!"

Joy gave me a thumbs-up.

When we got to the dance studio, a woman came to greet us at the front desk. She wore black tights, a long-sleeve leotard, and a long black skirt. Her hair was up in a bun.

"Welcome to the studio!" she said. "I'm Madame Juliette."

I smiled. "I'm Lola," I replied. "And this is Joy. We're here for ballet. It's our first day."

"Ballet is in the blue room," Madame Juliette told us. "Follow me."

Madame Juliette led the way down a long hallway lined with cubbies. "Next time you come in, you can leave your things here," she told us. "Then come into this room."

We walked into a studio with blue walls. There were other kids already standing at a long double barre. They were all wearing tights and leotards.

"You two will be behind Ruth," Madame Juliette said, pointing to a girl with red hair. "Everyone, meet Lola and Joy. This is their first lesson."

Ruth waved at us. Joy and I went to stand behind her at the barre. Madame Juliette walked over to us.

"There are five foot positions in ballet," she explained. She motioned to a poster that showed them. "We will start in first position. Heels together, toes apart."

I looked down and put my heels together, making a V with my feet.

"Most ballet terms are in French," Madame Juliette continued. "With time, you'll learn them. For now, try to follow along as we go."

I looked at Joy. She smiled back at me. We were going to be great!

"Everyone, first position. Demi-plié—bend your knees—one-two. Relevé—up on your

tiptoes—three-four . . ." Madame Juliette started.

Joy and I watched the other dancers and copied their moves. It didn't seem hard at all. I was already a ballerina!

We did the same moves on both sides, and then the music stopped.

"Ruth, please demonstrate the tendu," said Madame Juliette. "With tendu, you want to imagine your toes are drawing a straight line on the floor . . ."

I only half listened as Madame explained the move. Ruth moved her foot to the front, side, back.

Ballet is easy! I thought. I could already picture myself leaping gracefully across the stage.

Suddenly the music started playing. I realized I hadn't been paying attention.

What was a tendu? I wondered. *Should I ask Madame to repeat it?*

But we were already moving on to the next move.

"Next glissade—a gliding step," Madame called. "Ruth, please show the class."

I'll figure it out, I decided. *I'm a great dancer.*

Ruth started doing the combination. I got distracted looking at all the beautiful ballerina pictures on the wall.

The music started up again. I turned back and tried to follow along. It was a little harder than I'd thought.

"We always finish barre with the grand battement. Start in fifth position with your heel touching your toe," Madame Juliette said.

I watched Ruth to see what she did.

"Watch how she kicks up hard and then lowers her leg as soft as a feather," Madame said. "Now everyone else. Two front, two side, two back, two side. "

Two, two, two, two. "That sounds like tutu!" I whispered to Joy.

She giggled. "I can't wait to wear a tutu on stage," she whispered back.

The music started playing again. Joy and I tried to follow along. But instead of going to the back, Joy started going to the front. We accidentally kicked each other.

Madame Juliette hurried over. "Are you okay, girls?" she asked. "You need to pay attention to the steps and count. We don't want any accidents."

Joy and I both blushed, but we nodded.

Madame turned on the music. I tried to pay attention, but I started thinking about the Latin rhythms we'd listened to in the car. They were stuck in my head! I started shaking my hips to the beat in my mind.

Madame Juliette stopped the music and stood in front of me.

"No, no, no. Your hips need to be square, Lola," she told me. "We don't shake our hips in ballet."

Everyone stared in my direction. I felt embarrassed.

I looked at the clock. Ten more minutes to go. It felt more like ten hours! But finally, class was over.

"Bye, girls! I hope you enjoyed the class. See you Wednesday," Madame Juliette said.

Joy and I waved and left as fast as we could. Mama was waiting outside to take us home.

"How was class?" she asked.

Joy and I exchanged a look.

"Not good," I grumbled. "Ballet is hard! And the music we were listening to in the car got stuck in my head. I started shaking my hips in the middle of class. Madame Juliette stopped the music to correct me. It was so embarrassing!"

"It was your first class ever, and you're learning," Mama said. "I'm sure your teacher was trying to help." She glanced at Joy. "Joy, did you like it?"

Joy shook her head. "No, I accidentally kicked Lola, and I was so uncomfortable. Whoever invented tights was not kidding. They are tight!"

"I don't think I'm cut out for ballet," I said.

"Ballet takes work and practice. You can't give up after one class," Mama said.

I sighed. I'd been so excited for ballet, but one class was one too many. What had I done?

Chapter 4

No More Ballet!

Ballet was *not* for me! Being a ballerina was not as fun as watching a dance performance.

"I don't want to go back to ballet today," I told Mama after school on Wednesday.

"Lola, I know your first class wasn't perfect, but today is a new day. It might take a few lessons for you to feel comfortable. Give it time," Mama said.

I sighed. "Do I have to?" I asked.

"Yes," Mama said firmly. "You made a commitment. Life sometimes gets hard, but it doesn't mean you quit. Now, go get dressed."

I went upstairs and wiggled into my tights and leotard. When I came back downstairs, Mama was video chatting with Abuelita.

"¡Hola, Lola!" Abuelita said. "How was your first ballet class?"

"Hard!" I said. "I thought it would be more about pretty costumes and shiny tiaras. But all the steps have weird names. It's nothing like dancing at home."

Abuelita chuckled. "Hard work is good for the body and mind. If you stick with it, ballet will be fun!"

I was not convinced. Mama and Abuelita seemed to be, though. I agreed to give dance another try.

Mama and I said goodbye to Abuelita. Then we drove to Joy's house to pick her up.

"Sorry," Joy said when she got in the car. She was a little out of breath. "It took me a long time to put on my tights. When I got done, they were inside out!"

I frowned. Mama had said today was a new day, but so far it was not off to a good start.

At the studio, Joy and I left our bags in the cubbies and went to our class. We lined up at the barre.

Like before, we started with demi-plié and relevé. I made sure to follow along more closely. I didn't want to be embarrassed again.

No hip shaking! I reminded myself.

Thankfully, the moves seemed a little easier today. It was still hard work, but I didn't feel as lost as the first day.

Finally, Madame Juliette announced it was grand battement. I knew that meant we were almost done with the barre. Joy and I were careful not to kick each other this time.

As we were stretching, Madame made an announcement.

"Each season, the studio puts on a recital," she said. "This time, we are going to do a special performance of *Swan Lake*."

Everyone cheered. We were all excited for a performance.

That means we'll get sparkly tiaras and tutus!
I thought. I shared an excited grin with Joy.

"Just like the show we saw!" she whispered.

"Since we have some time left, we will watch
a bit of *Swan Lake*," Madame Juliette said. She
turned on the TV.

"*Swan Lake* is about a prince who is told
he must marry," Madame explained as the
performance started on-screen. "While hunting,
he discovers a swan lake. For our performance,
the prince will be guided by two chickens."

"Chickens!" someone said. We all giggled.

Madame laughed too. "I'm serious!" she said. "There are a limited number of swan roles. I want to give everyone a chance to show their feathers. Our performance will be a bit different. We will have chickens as part of the cast too."

She turned back to the TV. The swans, wearing the most beautiful dresses, were dancing gracefully.

"The prince learns that the swans turn human after dark," she explained. "An evil sorcerer keeps them captive. The prince is about to announce his love for the princess."

Madame Juliette looked at her watch. "We're out of time for today," she said, turning off the TV. "I'll announce performance roles during our next class."

I didn't need to wait until the next class to learn my role. I knew what I was going to be—a swan!

Chapter 5

The Big Reveal

"I can't wait for Madame Juliette to tell us our roles," I said when Mama and I picked up Joy on Friday. "We're going to be the best swans!"

"I want to wear a beautiful tutu," Joy cheered.

"Sign me up for a shiny tiara!" I exclaimed.

When we got to class, Madame Juliette took her place at the front of the studio. She held a piece of paper in her hands.

"Attention," she said. "Please listen as I read the names for the cast."

She listed the dancers who would have roles in the castle and village first. Then it was time for the swans!

"Fingers crossed!" I told Joy.

Madame started reading again. "Ruth, Fran, Briana, Eloise . . ."

She read a lot of names. My heart was racing.

"Lola . . ." Madame Juliette paused.

"Yes, I would love to be a swan!" I cheered.

Madame shook her head. "I'm sorry, Lola. You're still a beginner. You'll be a chicken with

Joy. But it is a very important role. You'll be guiding the prince."

I couldn't believe it. I must have heard wrong.

"Chickens?" I whispered to Joy.

Joy nodded. She had tears in her eyes.

"We got the wrong feathers!" I protested.

Only Joy heard me. The rest of our classmates were celebrating. Everyone else seemed happy about their roles.

What about our tiaras or beautiful tutus? I thought sadly.

I wanted to dance gracefully like a swan. Instead, Joy and I would be hopping and flapping like chickens. This was a disaster!

Chapter 6

Wrong Feathers

I was quiet on the ride home. After we dropped off Joy, Mama turned to me.

"You're too quiet, Lola. What happened at dance?" she asked.

I sighed. "Madame announced our roles for the recital. I'm not going to be a swan. I'm going to be a chicken!" I wailed.

"Oh, mija, I'm sorry. I know how much you wanted to be a swan." Mama paused. "But all roles are important. And you'll have the chance to learn and perform either way."

What am I going to learn from being a chicken? I thought.

When we got home, I went upstairs to my room. I didn't want to talk to anyone.

"Lola, dinner is ready!" Mama hollered from the kitchen awhile later.

I shuffled downstairs. Dad, Mama, and Mariana were already at the table.

"Why the long face?" Dad asked. "Something ruffling your feathers?"

Mama shook her head. I did not laugh.

"I'm sorry you're unhappy, Lola, but chickens are funny." Dad took a bite of his dinner. "And tasty!" he added with a wink.

I giggled. Dad could always make me laugh.

"You know, Abuelita used to have pet chickens at la finca—the farm—growing up," Mama said. "Why don't you call her? You might change your mind about being a chicken."

I didn't think that was likely, but Abuelita always made me feel better. And she always had the best stories. After dinner, I called her.

"Your mama told me today was a big day for you," Abuelita said. "Any news?"

I sighed. "I'll be a chicken!"

Abuelita chuckled. "There are no chickens at the swan lake!"

"There are in this show," I said. "Madame Juliette created extra roles so everyone could have a part."

"A special role? How wonderful!" Abuelita exclaimed.

"It's not wonderful. It's embarrassing!"

"The role is what you make it," Abuelita told me.

I sighed. "I wanted to have feathers, but not chicken feathers."

"Chickens are fun animals. I used to have pollos—chickens—growing up," Abuelita told me. "Every single one had its own personality! Once I had a chicken that liked walking backward. Another hated mud. She would tiptoe around like she was dancing."

I giggled. That was funny to imagine.

"You can be a team player, even when you don't have a lead part, Lola. Every single

person in the production is important," Abuelita pointed out.

"Even a chicken?" I asked.

"If you love what you are doing, the audience will see it," Abuelita said. "I can't wait to see you perform. I'll have to ask your parents to record the recital."

"I'm worried people will laugh at me," I confessed.

"Don't pay attention to what other people think," Abuelita said. "If you are happy and comfortable in your own feathers, that's all that matters! Since your role is new, you can make it your own."

Maybe Abuelita had a point. It would be nice to be onstage with the lights and the music. I did love to dance. Ballet was different than dancing at home, but it was still fun.

I hung up feeling happy. I was going to work hard and make Abuelita proud!

Chapter 7

Costume Time

I kept thinking about Abuelita's words: *The role is what you make it.* But what could I make of a chicken?

At ballet, we were busy rehearsing for the show and learning new steps. My favorite was bourrée. We started in fifth position. Then we moved quickly back and forth on the balls of our feet. It reminded me of the backward chicken Abuelita had told me about.

Joy loved to leap and jump. Her favorite step was pas de chat.

"That means the step of the cat," Madame Juliette explained. "You leap from one leg to the other while drawing a diamond in the air with your legs."

With every class, we learned something new. I was working hard.

Madame Juliette noticed. "You are doing great, Lola! You're gaining flexibility and memorizing the steps. Good job!" she said.

"Thank you!" I replied.

At the end of class one afternoon, Madame clapped her hands to get our attention. "I have a surprise for everyone," she said with a smile. "Costumes!"

Joy looked at me. I knew she felt the same way I did—excited but nervous.

"Let's hope we get beautiful feathers!" I whispered to Joy.

Chicken costumes would not be as beautiful as swan costumes, but I remembered what Abuelita had told me. *Every single person in the production is important.*

Madame Juliette went through all the costumes. I almost thought she had forgotten about us.

"Last but not least, our chickens!"

Madame Juliette held out two costumes. They looked like sacks with feathers glued on. Madame handed us yellow tights and white leotards too.

"Thank you," I said quietly.

I tried to be positive. But all I could think about was how ridiculous we would look.

"Did you like our costumes?" I asked Joy as we left the room.

"No! Not one bit!" Joy said. "Everyone is going to laugh at us!"

"I told Abuelita the same thing," I said. "She told me, 'If you are happy and comfortable in your own feathers, that's all that matters.'"

"Why did the chicken cross the road?" Joy asked.

"Why?" I replied.

"To get away from the recital!" Joy exclaimed.

I laughed. "Abuelita said we need to be comfortable in our own feathers. But how can we do that in such embarrassing costumes?"

I thought for a minute. "Maybe we should talk to Madame Juliette."

Joy nodded. "Good idea."

We went back into the studio. Our teacher was still there.

"Madame Juliette, can we please talk to you for a few minutes?" I asked.

"Sure, girls. What's going on?" she replied.

"We don't want to be chickens," I confessed.

"And we really don't like our costumes," Joy added.

Madame sighed. "I know everyone wants to be a swan. But this is your first year dancing. It takes years of practice to land a lead role. I created these roles for you. I see how hard you're working. You have potential."

"But we're just chickens," I said.

"You're not *just* chickens," Madame corrected. "Without you, the prince won't go to the forest. He'll never find the swan lake!"

"So we're not just in the background?" Joy asked.

"Not at all! Don't get discouraged. Keep working hard, and with every performance, you have a chance of getting a better role," Madame Juliette said.

I nodded. That made sense. But still . . .

"Can we do anything about our costumes?" I asked.

"Tell you what. Why don't you think of some ways to make them more fun?" Madame suggested. "We can talk about it during our next class."

Joy and I agreed. We left the studio feeling a little better. Now we just had to figure out what to do with our costumes. . . .

Chapter 8

A Great Idea

I was still thinking about my costume that weekend.

"I think you'll be a cute chicken," Mama said when I told her about it. "And in the meantime, you can do your chores. I need you to help me dust the living room."

I grabbed a feather duster. Abuelita's stories about the funny chickens on the farm came to my mind. I imagined being a chicken with fluffy feathers. I held the duster up to my head.

"What are you doing, Lola?" Mama asked.

"Research!" I replied with a giggle. "I'm getting into character as a chicken."

Mama laughed. "I have the perfect song for you!" She put on the chicken dance.

"*Cluck, cluck!*" I said.

Mariana clucked with me. We giggled.

"You see, being a chicken can be fun!"
Mama said.

That gave me an idea. "Could we make
feather headpieces to go with our costumes?"
I asked. "That would make them way more
fun."

"That's a great idea! Why don't you ask
Madame Juliette first?" Mama said. "If she
says it's okay, I'll help you make them."

On our way to ballet later that week, I told Joy my idea.

"Maybe you can come over after class one day," I said. "We can create headpieces!"

"That would be so cool!" Joy agreed.

Before class started, Joy and I walked up to our teacher.

"Madame Juliette, we came up with an idea for our costumes," I said.

"What do you have in mind?" Madame replied.

"Can we make feather headpieces to help us stand out?" I asked.

"Maybe they could even have some glitter and jewels?" Joy added. "We'll look like extra fancy chickens that way."

Madame nodded. "Great idea! I love that you're getting into it and owning your roles."

"Thank you!" I said with a giant smile. Now that we were owning our feathers, things were looking up!

Chapter 9

Master Creation

That weekend, Joy came over to work on our headpieces. Mama had all the supplies ready for us at the kitchen table.

"I got feathers from the craft store, plus headbands, jewels, and extra glitter," she said.

"Thank you, Mama," I replied.

Joy and I got to work. It was a bit tricky at first. The feathers wouldn't stick to the headbands.

"We need the hot glue gun," Mama announced. She helped us hot-glue the feathers in place.

"Time to decorate!" Joy exclaimed.

"We need to let them dry first," Mama explained.

While our headpieces dried, Joy and I rehearsed in the living room. Mama and Mariana came to watch us.

"Bourrée for sixteen counts. Then we turn and bourrée for sixteen counts in the other direction," I said.

"This is the part where we are guiding the prince to the forest!" Joy said.

"Pas de chat, pas de chat," I repeated, just like Madame had taught us.

Mariana giggled and clapped. I giggled too. Being a chicken was actually fun!

"My grandparents, aunts, and uncles are coming to watch the show," Joy announced when we took a break.

"My parents will be there too," I said. "My dad is going to record the show for the rest of the family in Guatemala."

"We're going to be celebrities!" Joy joked.

"Ready to decorate?" Mama asked.

We went back to the kitchen table to work.

"What do you think about this?" Joy asked. She showed me a beautiful, feathered headpiece.

"Maybe some more glitter?" I suggested. "Extra glitter can't hurt!" I held up my headpiece. "Do you like mine?"

Joy nodded. "Maybe a few more jewels," she said.

We kept working until we had the most amazing chicken headpieces ever!

"Now we need to see if they stay together," I said.

Joy and I put on our headpieces and went back to the living room. We leaped, twirled, and bowed. Not a single feather fell out of place.

Joy and I high-fived. We couldn't wait to wear our creations onstage. Being a chicken was going to be awesome!

Chapter 10

Recital

We kept rehearsing. Abuelita was right. Ballet was hard work, but it was a lot of fun.

Finally, it was showtime! Joy and I got dressed backstage with the rest of our class. Even though the swan costumes were beautiful, I was happy as a chicken.

"You look amazing!" I said to Joy.

"Love the feathers!" she replied.

We peeked out from behind the curtains. It was a full house!

For a moment, I was nervous. It felt like when I was the new kid at school, and I had to do a presentation in front of the class.

What if I mess up and everyone laughs at me? I worried.

I remembered Abuelita's words. *Don't pay attention to what other people think. If you are happy and comfortable in your own feathers, that's all that matters!*

Madame Juliette called us to line up. "Places everyone!" she said.

The lights dimmed, and the music started. It felt just like the show I had seen for my birthday. I couldn't believe I was going to *be* one of the ballerinas onstage this time.

"Break a leg, girls!" Madame Juliette whispered with a smile.

I grabbed Joy's hand, and we went to our spot. Just before the curtain went up, Joy squeezed my hand.

"We can do this!" I whispered.

The curtain went up, and the lights came on. They were so bright I couldn't see the audience in front of me.

Joy and I launched into our routine. Bourrée, turn, walk, walk, pas de chat.

We leaped and twirled across the stage. Our feathery headpieces sparkled as we danced.

When we landed on our final pose, the music stopped. We bowed, and I heard clapping and cheering.

"Bravo, Lola!" I heard my dad's voice.

"Amazing, Joy!" someone else shouted.

The rest of the show was a success. Backstage, everyone was excited.

"Great job, girls!" Madame Juliette said.

Our families came backstage too. I felt like a famous ballerina!

"I'm so proud of you both!" Mama told us.

"You were outstanding, girls!" said Joy's mom. "I loved your headpieces."

"We made them ourselves!" I announced proudly.

Being a chicken isn't so bad after all, I thought. Especially now that I was comfortable in my own feathers.

GLOSSARY

archaeologist (ar-kee-OL-uh-jist)—a person who learns about the past by digging up old buildings or objects and studying them

barre (BAR)—a wooden bar dancers use for balance

bourrée (boo-REY)—a gliding move across the floor

chore (CHOR)—a job that must be done regularly

glissade (gli-SAHD)—a sliding or gliding step

grand battement (GRAND BAT-munt)—a dance move where one leg is straightened and kicked forward, to the side, or behind

hobby (HOB-ee)—something that you enjoy doing in your extra time

orchestra (OR-kuh-struh)—a large group of musicians who perform together

pas de chat (pah duh SHA)—a jump of one foot over the other

plié (plee-EY)—a move in which a dancer bends his or her knees while keeping the back straight

program (PROH-gram)—a thin book or a piece of paper that gives information about a performance

recital (ri-SIE-tuhl)—a dance performance

relevé (rel-uh-VEY)—to rise up onto the toes from a flat foot

tendu (than-DOO)—stretching the foot and leg from one position to another while keeping it on the floor

tradition (truh-DISH-uhn)—a custom, idea, or belief passed down through time

SPANISH GLOSSARY

abuelita (ah-bweh-LEE-tah)—grandmother

abuelo (ah-BWEH-loh)—grandfather

adiós (ah-dee-OHS)—goodbye

felicidades (feh-lee-see-DAH-dehs)—congratulations

feliz cumpleaños (FUH-leez koom-pleh-AH-nyohs)—happy birthday

hola (OH-lah)—hi or hello

la finca (lah FEENG-kah)—the farm

mija (MEE-ha)—Spanish for "my daughter" but can also be used as a term of affection meaning "my child," "dear," or "honey"

pollo (POH-yoh)—chicken

te quiero (tay KYEH-roh)—I love you

tres leches (trehs LEH-chehs)—cake made of three different types of milk

ya queremos pastel (YAH ke-RER-mohs pahs-TEHL)—we want cake

TALK ABOUT IT

1. Lola, Joy, and Sophia all enjoy different hobbies. Do you have any hobbies, like playing a sport or an instrument? Talk about your favorite hobby, how you got started with it, and what you like about it.

2. Do you think Lola was right to want to quit ballet? Why or why not? Talk about some other ways she could have handled the situation.

3. Look back through this story at the different advice Abuelita gives Lola. What do you think is the most useful? Talk about your choice.

WRITE IT DOWN

1. Do you like to dance? If so, write a paragraph about what type of dance you enjoy. If not, write about a type of dance you would like to learn. (It can be ballet or something else.)

2. Abuelita tells Lola a story about the chickens she had growing up on la finca—the farm. Write your own story using one of the chickens as a starting point.

3. Mama asks Lola to help her with chores, like dusting. What are some things you help with at home? Make a list of your chores and responsibilities.

MAKE A FEATHER HEADPIECE

Lola and Joy create feather headpieces to make their chicken costumes stand out. Try making your own headpiece—don't forget to be comfortable in your own feathers!

WHAT YOU NEED

- 1-inch-wide headband
- hot glue gun
- glue stick or liquid glue
- glitter, jewels, and feathers (can be one color or different colors)
- bobby pins